THE GHOSTLY NIGHT

A Cannoli Cafe Cozy Mystery

LIZZIE BENTON

http://lizziebenton.com

ALSO BY LIZZIE BENTON

Cannoli Cafe Mystery Series

Murder and Macaroons

Murder and Macaroni

Iced Cookie Murder

Murder and Bubbly

Murder, Purder

The Executive

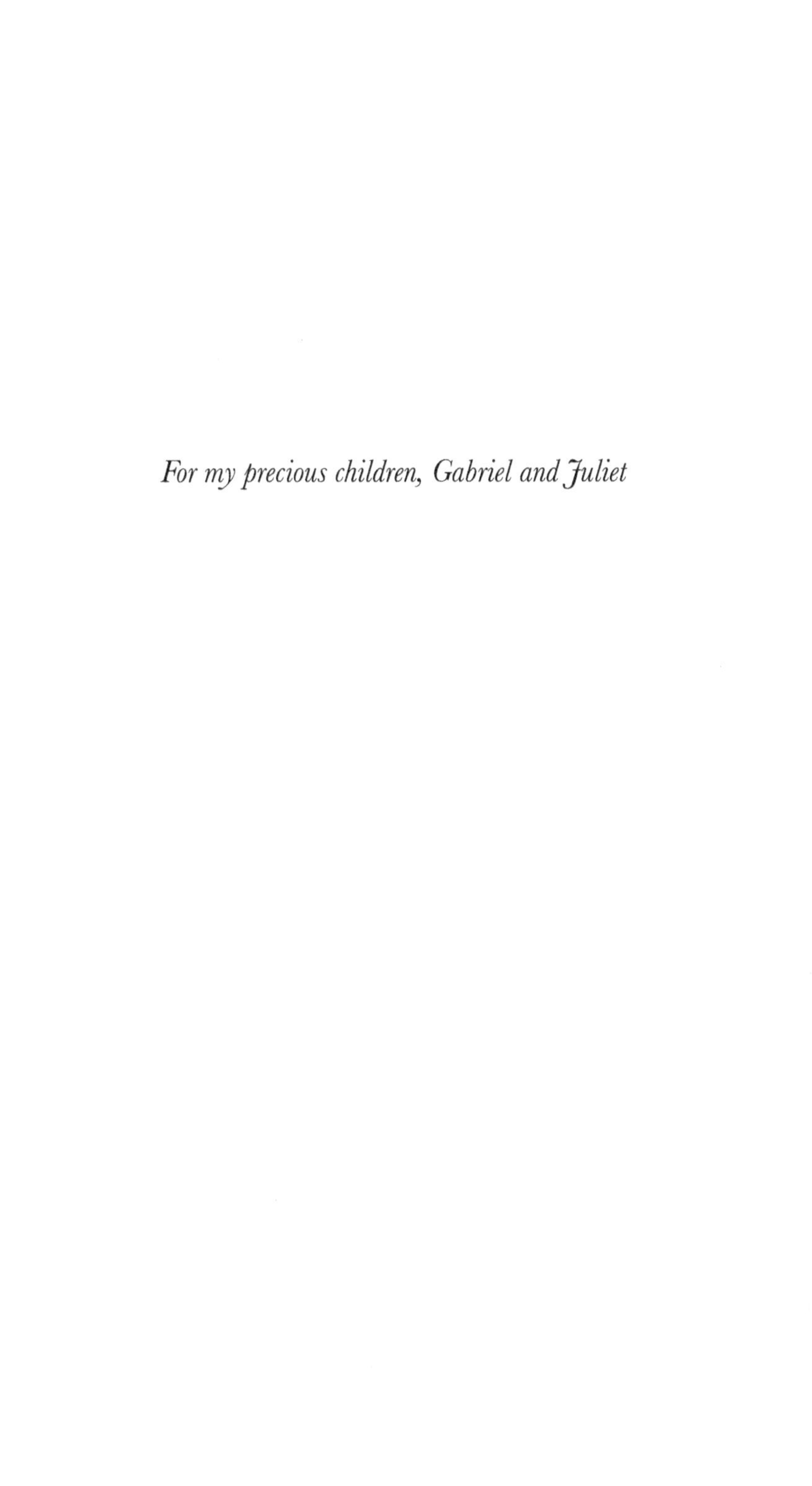

For my precious children, Gabriel and Juliet

APRIL 22, 1923

Jack Dixon was about to die. He knew, deep inside his heart of hearts, the inevitable was only minutes away. *If only*, he pondered.

"No!" shouted Jack aloud as he slammed his fist down on top of his ornate wooden desk and grunted loudly. He had always suspected his time would come to a premature end, but he never expected it would be this early. A dark and stormy evening that April in 1923, the owner of Rosewood's general store — Dixon's Goods and Wares — jumped out of his chair and feverishly paced in his study, located inside his beautiful Victorian home in the town next door — Waterford, New Jersey. The rain pounded the roof above him, and the ground below him. "No, no, no!" he yelled, as he abruptly stopped pacing in front of the fireplace. With red, bloodshot eyes, he stared into the crackling flames, losing himself in his wild, untamed thoughts as he considered all scenarios and possibilities. Jack gripped the mantle firmly, an attempt to stabilize himself and his thoughts. Was there any way to prevent his own murder? He wondered.

Shaking his head, Jack stumbled over to his desk once again, and eyed the paper he had written three names on a few minutes prior. He knew one of the three would murder him that night, but the question was: Who would deal the final blow? Was it his wife, Melba Dixon? Or his business partner, Frederick Clemmons? He shook his head, unsure. Perhaps it was someone he would have never expected prior to recent events — his store clerk, Herman Hammond? Jack sighed. He was quite *certain* he was about to be killed by one of his dearest friends, or his wife, and that it was about to happen imminently. Lightning flashed outside the windows, and thunder boomed in the distance. Jack closed his eyes as tears appeared on his cheeks, feelings of fright and dread consuming him.

Suddenly, the door flew open. A cloaked figure dashed to the fireplace and grabbed two heavy candlesticks from the mantle with gloved hands. All in black, the figure truly appeared as Death itself. As Jack Dixon turned to run out of the room, the figure jumped in front of him and swung the heavy candlesticks into Jack's head, knocking him straight to the floor.

And then, Jack Dixon was no more.

CHAPTER ONE

"How exciting, Nicole and Lia! So, when are you two planning to open up your new bed-and-breakfast?" asked Neelam. She twirled her long, black hair between her fingers as she sat beside Lia at the sparkling counter inside the Cannoli Cafe. The chemical engineer turned Cannoli Cafe owner, Nicole, gripped the handle tightly on the espresso machine on the other side of the counter, opposite Lia and Neelam, as she frothed the milk for their three cappuccinos. The cafe smelled heavenly, with the bright aroma of freshly brewed coffee enveloping the customers, as the sun glowed through the large windows. It was summer in Rosewood, New Jersey, and Nicole was not only off for the summer from teaching chemical engineering courses part-time at the University of New Jersey, but she was actually off indefinitely. And that felt so odd to her.

"We expect to open our new bed-and-breakfast as soon as we're done with the renovations, hopefully next month!" answered Nicole as she served her two friends their cappuccinos.

Nicole's mind wandered to everything that had occurred the past year as she prepared a plate full of macaroon cookies from behind the counter. She and Lia had purchased a fixer-upper Victorian home, just over the border in Waterford, as an investment property — to become their future bed-and-breakfast. Nicole cringed when she considered what else had happened around the time Nicole and Lia found their investment property — mainly, the surreal reunion with their childhood friend, Neelam (now sipping a cappuccino directly across from her), as they had attempted to figure out who tried to murder Neelam's husband, Dev, following his shocking collapse inside Nicole's Cannoli Cafe. As Nicole pushed the plate full of macaroon cookies in front of the trio of friends, her mind traveled even further back in time to all the ups and downs she had experienced with her beau, Dean. She winced. *What a year indeed*, thought Nicole.

"Thanks, Nicole," said Lia as she grabbed a macaroon cookie, complete with multicolored pignoli nuts on top. Lia was an accountant in Rosewood and owned her own practice there; she was also Nicole's longtime best friend from childhood. "Nicole, did you hear from your cousins, the Sorria sisters, yet?" asked Lia with her wide hazel eyes.

"I'm waiting for Maria and Amy Sorria to text me back. They should visit any day now to see the Victorian house we're renovating. They are looking forward to getting a preview of what Rosewood-Waterford life will be like once they head back to the area," answered Nicole. Realizing Neelam probably did not understand what her cousins had to do with their new bed-and-breakfast, Nicole turned to Neelam and explained, "My cousins are actually going to help manage the bed-and-breakfast for us, so that Lia can keep running her accounting practice and I can continue to manage the cafe here in Rosewood." She paused. "And maybe I will finally get back to writing that novel, eventually!" The three ladies laughed.

In truth, Nicole was not sure how much time she would really have once the bed-and-breakfast was open, especially since she was nervous about taking on another business, besides the cafe, but she hoped to eventually return to her hobby of writing now that she was freed up from the many hours that go into teaching at a university; even though she had been teaching part-time, many hours of preparation went into her weekly class, including answering numerous panicked emails from her students about the difficulty of the course material. Perhaps now, instead of writing emails, she could write her own book — both figuratively and literally. The only problem was, she still felt that pang in her heart about leaving the university; she especially felt heartbroken to leave the students who not only relied on her for guidance in their up-and-coming careers, but who also adored her. She sighed.

Nicole stopped her train of thought, realizing she had to focus on the projects in front of her, not on the university behind her. Grounding herself, she brought her cappuccino mug to her lips, tasting the bitterness of the espresso against the frothy texture of the milk, and took in the sight in front of her; she was indeed grateful to see her best friend and now business partner, Lia, sitting alongside their other old friend, Neelam — both with wide grins and happy eyes. It was important to count her blessings and acknowledge her dear friendships, and Nicole knew she could count on them to help her navigate the uncertain months in front of her. She smiled and relaxed her shoulders, feeling a bit more at ease.

"Professor, where's my spaghetti!" shouted Mr. Don Martini. His booming, firm voice startled the ladies. Then, the whole cafe erupted in laughter. Mr. Martini was one of Nicole's dear regulars. What started out as a weekly routine of playing chess with his friend Max in the Knights Chess Club, an organization which frequented the cafe as their primary playing location, turned into a daily habit.

"Coming right up, Mr. Martini!" said Nicole with a huge grin, shaking her head in amusement. Susie, Nicole's baker and manager, appeared with a tray bearing a bowl of spaghetti and handed it to Nicole. She winked as she handed it to Nicole, and Nicole smiled in gratitude. As Nicole made her way across her cafe, other customers nodded and grinned at her, including the Knitting for Good ladies (and gossipers) Doris, Mary, and Charlotte — clearly enjoying their time in the cozy establishment. Many small bistro-type tables lined the interior — as well as some larger, rectangular or circular tables for sizable groups.

"Here you go, Mr. Martini. Max, can I get you

anything?" asked Nicole as she placed the bowl on the table near the chess board. When she didn't get an immediate answer, she figured he was deep in concentration about the game in front of him. Somehow, chess was akin to life or death for the old men. "So, who's winning?" she asked.

Max shook his head. "Who do you think?" He frowned momentarily and then gave Nicole a wink, clearly shaking himself out of his disappointment.

"I got him good this time, Nicole. Real good!" said Mr. Don Martini. He raised his fisted hand in the air and shook it. Typically, when a scene like this occurred in the cafe, everyone would erupt in laughter. This time, however, the cafe was silent, to Nicole's surprise. Then, Nicole heard the front door close and noticed everyone's gaze was fixed on the entrance. She turned around to find Mayor Diane Eckel entering the cafe, to Nicole's surprise. Nicole hardly ever saw the mayor, as the mayor typically had her assistant pick up coffees to go on her behalf, but she had crossed paths occasionally with her — especially now that Nicole and Lia were on her Downtown Management Team as business owners. "Excuse me, gentlemen." Nicole made her way to the front of her establishment.

"Mayor Eckel! What a surprise? Is everything okay? Can I get you anything?" asked Nicole.

"Nicole, I'm afraid we need to talk. We have a problem," said the mayor.

Uh oh, thought Nicole. *Another murder?*

CHAPTER TWO

"WHAT A BEAUTIFUL SUMMER DAY! Right, ladies? Not too hot, and just right!" The mayor looked over at Neelam and Lia at the counter. "May I sit with you all? I'd like to run a few things by you."

Perplexed, Nicole furrowed her eyebrows. "I'm sorry, didn't you just say there is a problem? Did you hear something from the Waterford mayor? Is it about the bed-and-breakfast?" asked Nicole. A million things ran through Nicole's mind just then. Typically calm, she was beginning to feel more agitated about taking on this new business.

"First, priorities. A cappuccino would be divine. And one of those delish cannolis with the divine chocolate sauce, as well!" said the mayor, winking at Nicole.

"Yes, of course." Nicole nodded to Susie behind the counter, and Susie got straight to work.

The mayor, wearing a sharp skirt-suit, made her way to the stool nearest Lia. Nicole then positioned herself behind the counter so she could stand across from the three women.

"Can we help you with something, Mayor Eckel?" asked Lia. Lia glanced at Nicole, and Nicole was grateful for her friend's help in picking up the pace. The suspense was killing her.

Susie slid the cappuccino in front of the mayor. "As a matter of fact, that's just what I want to speak with all of you about. But before that—" the mayor paused, and Nicole's eyes widened and her heart stopped as she waited for another one of the mayor's stalled moments. Mayor Diane Eckel continued. "Let me welcome you back to town, Neelam! I'm so glad to hear you're moving to Rosewood from the city, and that you and your husband are opening a toy store in town, to boot!" said Mayor Eckel before she took a sip of her cappuccino.

Neelam brightened at the mayor's words. "Yes, thank you! The silver lining to the attempted murder of my husband Dev not long ago. Was he sitting on this very stool when he collapsed?"

Neelam paused as the other three women took in a breath at Neelam's reference to the moment everyone thought Dev collapsed and died inside the Cannoli Cafe.

Nicole just about mustered a response to her question. "Y-y-y-es!"

Neelam continued. "Terrible. Anyway, despite the attempt on Dev's life, we felt inspired to return to this cozy little town! Dev and I are renting an apartment right now. And we love the schools here. In fact, little Jason transferred into the first grade at the end of the school year. And we're waiting to close on the house we selected!" All three women stared at Neelam with wide eyes. Nicole, despite the tension she had previously been feeling related to the mayor's entrance, was now distracted with talk of Dev's attempted murder. Then she almost laughed to herself, thinking about the differences between her two friends Lia and Neelam. They were both bold in a way, but each presented their boldness differently. Lia was bold in a funny, spunky way, especially with her jokes. On the other hand, Neelam was fairly straightforward and opinionated at times, typically showing a direct, and sometimes even angry, side. A pharmaceutical company executive, Neelam was used to being strong and decisive.

Bringing up the horrific attempted murder of her husband just now was another example of how Neelam never hid circumstances and addressed everything head-on. Nicole suspected she'd see even more of Neelam's direct, business-like approach in the following months, the more comfortable she would become as she settled back into life in Rosewood, New Jersey.

Mayor Eckel nodded her head emphatically and beamed. "Well, I just want you to know how welcome you are, Neelam. I am so pleased at your decision, despite your circumstances—" The mayor's voice trailed off briefly as she said the last part very softly. "And Neelam, please be sure to attend the next Downtown Management Team meeting with Lia and Nicole." The mayor paused to taste a morsel of the cannoli Susie must have placed in front of her while they were all distracted with talk of Dev's collapse. "Oh, I also have one more favor to ask you ladies — that problem I mentioned," said Mayor Diane Eckel.

Nicole wrinkled her eyebrows. "Yes?" Finally, the moment Nicole was waiting for.

"Can you please reach out to Beth? She's done a wonderful job the past two years with her store, Beth's Boutique, but she hasn't gotten to know many people here since she moved here from Pennsylvania. Do you think you can reach out to her and encourage her to come to the meeting? You know me, I'm all about women's power, and I want you all running the show in town!" said Mayor Eckel. She flicked her head from side-to-side, clearly proud of the economic and diverse development of the downtown.

Nicole glanced at Lia. "This is the problem you spoke of, Mayor Eckel?"

"This cannoli is delicious, by the way," said the mayor. "Well, yes! Because Beth has not been coming to the meetings, and we're missing out on her talent and insight! I need your help to get her to the meetings."

Nicole considered what the mayor had asked. Beth was certainly an interesting person, in Nicole's view. Quiet and somewhat reserved, she was hard to get to know. But she seemed kind, and she ran a beautiful boutique full of children's clothes. It was hard for a small town retail store to make it these days, so Beth's success truly impressed Nicole. In fact, it actually made sense that Neelam and Dev were opening the toy store next door to Beth's Boutique, now that more people were visiting Rosewood from out-of-town to shop for children's clothes. It definitely seemed like a win-win to have a children's toy store alongside a children's clothing boutique.

"Of course. We'll visit with Beth and ask her to join us at the next meeting," answered Nicole.

"Great! I knew I could count on you ladies!" The major took a last sip of her drink. The dish with the cannoli was already completely empty. "Add it to my tab? I've got to run!" And before they knew it, she was out the door.

"I know I'm new, in a way. But that was bizarre," said Neelam.

"You don't know the half of it. The father of her son was murdered not that long ago. It's very complicated. She's been through a lot," said Nicole, thinking back to the first murder case she got involved with when she returned to Rosewood.

"Interesting visit indeed," said Lia. "Funny about her interest in Beth. I wonder if there's more to the story. And, you know, I always feel like there's a lot on Beth's mind every time I see those big, beautiful blue eyes of hers." Lia paused. "I suppose we should make more of an effort to get to know her, and help her feel more welcome."

"I agree. Maybe there is a lot on her mind, especially since it's difficult to run an old-fashioned store in town, especially with the malls and, even worse, online shopping." Nicole mused. She sipped her cappuccino, sensing the steaminess against her lips. "Well, you never know what's going on in people's minds. Maybe it's more than her store. Just like we still need to solve, you know—" Nicole paused, thinking about how they still hoped to determine what really happened to Lia's parents, who were murdered years before.

"Indeed!" Suddenly, Lia jumped. "Oh! I'm getting a call from our contractor, Tommy." Lia paused as she lifted the phone to her ear. "Hi, Tommy… What?...A secret room in the attic?...Full of old photos?" Nicole's eyes widened as she overheard her best friend. Neelam turned her head, clearly curious, as well. "We'll be right there!" shouted Lia.

"What?" asked Nicole after Lia hung up. Lia was already making her way to the front door.

"Let's go. Tommy found a secret room in the attic, with loads of stuff!" said Lia.

Susie emerged again from the kitchen. "Be careful, my dears. I think I will close up here soon. They say a big storm is coming late afternoon! Don't get trapped at the house!" She warned. "There could be flooding, downed lines, and power failures!"

"Don't worry!" shouted Nicole as she ran past Susie to retrieve her things from the kitchen before returning to the main part of the cafe.

"Bye, Neelam. Tell Jason we say hello!" said Lia.

"Bye, ladies. Keep me posted and be careful! Something tells me you're about to get embroiled in yet another mystery," cautioned Neelam.

As they exited the cafe, they walked towards Lia's luxury SUV. "I can't wait to see this. Old photos? I bet it's Jack Dixon and his family, the original owner of the Victorian home," said Lia.

"Yeah. I was just thinking about that. You know, they never solved *the* most famous murder case in the county." Nicole paused as they neared Lia's vehicle. She brushed her wavy, brown hair back and turned to face Lia directly, staring into Lia's hazel eyes before asking, "Who killed Jack Dixon?"

"Who killed Jack Dixon indeed!" exclaimed Lia with bright eyes. "You know, I think we're about to find out!"

CHAPTER THREE

"Oh my, the water level in the riverbank is getting quite high!" said Nicole as they crossed over a small bridge. They had just left Rosewood and entered Waterford — the town next door, a riverfront community in New Jersey. Lia was driving them back to the Victorian house they were renovating in Waterford. Susie's warning came true, after all. The storm had begun, and suddenly the rain was coming down very hard on Lia's luxury SUV.

"I know. I can't wait until we get there. It's a little difficult to drive in this rain!" said Lia. *Whoosh, whoosh, whoosh.* She increased the speed on the windshield wipers. "I suppose it's too late to turn back now. Best bet is to get to the house and hang tight while the storm passes!"

As the wipers rapidly ran across the windshield in front of them, Nicole shuddered. She struggled to see in front of her, and was amazed her friend Lia was handling the stress of the storm so well. "Too bad Dean isn't here. He is much better at driving in the rain. But he's busy at the FBI in Washington, DC on that special assignment," said Nicole.

"What do you think he'll do once he's done with his latest assignment, Nicole?" asked Lia. "Do you think he'll truly retire and become a private investigator? And stay in Rosewood? Do you think he'll settle down, marry, and have a family with you?" asked Lia.

Nicole sighed. "I'm honestly not sure." And she really wasn't. Her tall, dark, and handsome beau, Dean, was a widower; his wife, Jane, had passed away from a terrible illness early in his career with the FBI. She knew Dean was scarred and shaken from Jane's passing, and in addition to that, they continued to struggle to connect at times. While she knew they both cared for each other, they always seemed to hold back, in a way. Yet, she really missed him right now. She desperately wanted to feel close — at least emotionally, and she sometimes wondered if she should make more of an overture.

Should she try to show him how much she cared about him? Maybe he just needed reassurance, even though he seemed like a tough, strong FBI guy. Maybe *she* was the problem, Nicole wondered. She closed her eyes and held her breath, feeling anxious about it all.

Pound, pound, pound!

Nicole sighed again as she listened to the rain pounding on the roof of Lia's vehicle. As she tried to peer out the window, she saw streams of water hugging the sides of the road. It was getting pretty treacherous out there. Nicole gripped the seat below her, attempting to feel a bit more grounded. This trip to their Victorian house had too quickly become a nightmare.

"Earth to Nicole? Keep talking, so I feel less stressed while driving!" urged Lia.

Nicole chuckled at Lia's remark. "I was just feeling guilty about my love triangle. Maybe I'm thinking too much of it, but Drew Blackburn, our lawyer, continues to call me or visit the cafe occasionally. I really think he may like me. I feel a little sick about it, because I enjoy the occasional conversation with him. He's just a lot more open and easier to get to know. I feel like I should know Dean better considering we've technically known him since high school, but I'm just not there yet. At least in terms of feeling very close to him, emotionally. Especially after the past year and all the secrets that came to light, even if it wasn't his fault. But sometimes I really wish we were closer."

Nicole shuddered as the image of Dean holding a dead Professor Stephanie Purder in his arms, crying out, shook her. That was probably the "straw that broke the camel's back" as they say. Somehow, after that incident, she struggled to recapture her feelings completely for Dean. She always had a tiny element of distrust from that point on. At the same time, though, she was hopeful that things would continue to move forward for her relationship with Dean, and perhaps his decision about his future in the FBI — and whether he retire in Rosewood as a private investigator or resume his career in Washington DC — would be the deciding factor for their future.

Suddenly, Nicole's phone rang. After viewing the caller ID, she said, "Oh? It's my friend Gabriel, the head of Information Technology at the University of New Jersey!"

"Hmm! Interesting! Go ahead and get it!" said Lia. "Listening to your university politics will keep me distracted!" Lia chuckled as she increased the wiper speed even more.

Nicole took in a deep breath before swiping the green button to take the call. "Hello, Gabriel? Is everything okay?" asked Nicole.

"Hi, Nicole. I'm fine. But did you see that posting? I hope you will consider applying?" asked Gabriel.

"What posting?" she asked. She suddenly felt alarm travel through her body. Nicole had just taken a break from the university. *What now?*

"This job is perfect for you, Nicole. It's right up your alley! The Chair of the chemical engineering department just posted a new Professor of Practice role!" said Gabriel. "Isn't that great?"

Nicole's heart sank. Why didn't the Chair or Assistant Chair of the department call her about it? They had previously discussed and brainstormed this exact role together in the past, but the university had never approved it before due to the budget (since it would pay more than what she had been doing part time). A Professor of Practice job was a teaching role much more interesting than the standard one she had been doing part time, since it would leverage both her industry and academic experiences — and required more strategy and creativity from a curriculum perspective. "But Gabriel, maybe the Chair created it for someone else? He *must* have someone else in mind, especially since I have not heard from him." A million thoughts swam through Nicole's head from the past year at the university, especially with all the politics she endured. She always struggled to decipher all the hints, winks, and false leads in academia, and it often stressed her out. Between the university and all the murders in Rosewood, Nicole certainly had a rough year.

"Nicole, I know you've got these business ventures going, especially with the new bed-and-breakfast on the horizon, but you could theoretically have people manage those for you. We miss you at the University of New Jersey. Besides, most importantly, I know a bunch of students who are missing out on learning from you; you know that's the most critical thing, and I know you can't turn your back on them. Why don't you apply?" asked Gabriel. "They need you! No one else can speak both languages of industry *and* academia. You know only *you* can do that." Gabriel's voice sounded deep. And serious.

Nicole's heart sank even further. They always knew how to affect her at the university, especially by bringing up students. She took in a deep breath. "Okay, I'll think about it. I promise I will take a look at the posting later, Gabriel. I do appreciate you telling me about it. We're actually driving now in the middle of the storm, Lia and me, so we can get to the Victorian property. Our contractor found a whole bunch of old photos and objects in the secret room in the attic!"

"Oh no. I know what that means," said Gabriel, laughing. "You're going to figure out who murdered that owner of the house, aren't you? Jack Dixon, is it?" asked Gabriel.

"I think that's where we're heading, but let's see once we examine all the contents of that room! Okay, Gabriel. Be careful in the storm! And thank you for letting me know. I'm sure everything will work out for the best. Let's see what happens."

"I agree, dear. Be careful!" said Gabriel. "And keep me posted! Bye now."

And then Nicole heard a click.

Just then, they pulled up to the low stone wall in front of the house. Nicole marveled at how beautiful the exterior now looked, even under dark skies. The exterior freshly painted, a bright mauve juxtaposed with light brown tones, certainly emphasized the house's dollhouse appearance, especially with the spacious front porch and beautiful terrace on the second floor — with views of the river. Rain still battering Lia's vehicle, they ran into the house and quickly closed the front door. "Whoa! What a trip!" said Lia. "By the way, you need to fill me in on all that university stuff later. Never a dull moment for you there! But right now, we need to see all the treasure in the secret room!" Lia grinned. Nicole was happy for the distraction, feeling very thrown off by Gabriel's call — in the middle of the storm, no less.

Suddenly, Tommy came running down the stairs, gripping the ornate railings on the way down. "I'm sorry, ladies. I gotta get out of here! This storm is getting out of control. You'll see when you go up the stairs. Go up to the third floor and look for a giant hole in the wall. You'll find the secret room now; you can't miss it!" Tommy opened the front door, wind gusting and rain hitting the pavement, hard. "I'll touch base with you ladies tomorrow. Be careful, and make sure you leave soon. Get home safely!" he yelled. As Tommy slammed the front door shut, Nicole could hear the rain beating on top of the house. She and Lia looked at each other. After removing their shoes — so they would not get the newly finished floors dirty — they ran up the stairs and followed Tommy's instructions. Just as Tommy said, when they got up to the third floor, there was a giant hole they could step through to get to the secret room.

Nicole glanced around once she finally caught her breath at the top of the steps. It looked like a scene from a movie. Many books, chests, and old candlesticks were visible from the giant hole in the wall. While the room before her was small and secret, she realized immediately that it held a treasure trove of information. As she looked over to her friend and investment partner, Lia, they nodded to one other. Time to cross over the threshold and find out what was in store for them! They each carefully stepped through the hole in the wall. And as Lia and Nicole crossed over and examined the room more carefully, they each mentally decided what to tackle next.

"Let's look at this chest over here!" said Lia. Lia crossed the room and opened the chest. Once she cracked the top of the chest open, she found a stack of letters bundled together on the right side! Both ladies' eyes widened at the sight. But as Lia and Nicole sat down to examine the letters, the lights and power suddenly went out in the entire house!

"Oh no!" exclaimed Nicole. Fortunately, Nicole

had one of those portable charging devices that included a flashlight inside her purse. Lia did, as well. They had both stocked up on them when they first bought the house, as it did not have electricity for a long time. Part of the renovations included rewiring and updating the house, so there was sufficient lighting. Nicole carefully felt for the opening of her purse and took the device out. Once her flashlight was on, Lia did the same with the aid of Nicole's light. With both powerful flashlights on, they were in business.

Just then, on their phones, they heard the emergency signal go off loudly. They each saw the notification that no one should go out on the roads due to downed lines and power failures.

"Well, I guess we might as well make ourselves comfortable! Why don't you go through this half of the stack, and I'll go through the other half? I wonder what we'll find!" said Lia. As Lia had been speaking, Nicole had peeked through the rest of the contents of that chest with her flashlight. She saw photos from the family of Jack Dixon. One photo had Jack, his wife, Melba, and their son, Robert. Another photo showed Jack with two of his associates. Nicole recalled the presentations from the Rosewood-Waterford Historical Society at the library; Jack Dixon's two associates were named Herman Hammond and Frederick Clemmons. She shuddered when she suddenly realized that Jack Dixon was most likely murdered by someone he knew very closely. *Perhaps it was one of these individuals in the photographs*, she thought. And as she considered that idea, she began to unravel and open the envelopes that were addressed to a woman named Lila Rose Parker — handed to her by her best friend, Lia.

Nicole pointed to the name and address of Lila Rose Parker to her friend and said, "Who's that?"

Lia, with her typical wide hazel eyes, said, "I have no idea!"

And then thunder suddenly boomed above them — shaking the house — and lightning flashed outside the attic windows as the wind howled.

What a night indeed!

CHAPTER FOUR

IN THE SHADOWY darkness of the attic, Lia and Nicole continued to sift through the letters exchanged between the unknown woman, Lila Rose Parker, and Jack Dixon, while gripping their flashlights. A haunting scene indeed, the house creaked loudly every time there was a large gust of wind. The crackles of thunder and flashcs of lightning were unrelenting as the two ladies pored over the contents inside the letters.

"Look, Nicole! Here's the letter that explains what all this is about!" said Lia.

Dear Robert,
 Your father and I had corresponded as

friends for many years. I had known him since childhood, and while we were betrothed to others, we remained good friends through our letters. I was so saddened to hear of his passing, or rather murder, all those years ago. I've always wondered who committed that unspeakable crime. Perhaps there is a clue hidden inside the bundle of letters I have sent you, exchanged between your father and me. Please take a look and see.

Best wishes, and sincerely,
Lila Rose Parker
August 20, 1985

Nicole squinted as she considered what Lia had just read to her. "I remember that Robert was Jack Dixon's son." She paused. "But what's interesting is that we purchased the house from a company that scoops up abandoned or foreclosed homes. I wonder how that happened — that we didn't buy it from the original family? And didn't Robert have children, and where did they go?" Nicole scratched her head, confused. Suddenly, thunder cracked in the distance once again.

"Nicole, it's 11 PM already! We had better get to bed. But it's certainly clear that we have a lot of work to do in discovering who truly murdered Jack Dixon, the original owner of this house!" Lia struggled to push herself off the floor. After attempting to gain her balance, and with Nicole's help, she stood up.

"You're right, Lia. But one thing is very interesting: Jack Dixon wrote quite a bit about his business partner, Frederick Clemmons, along with his clerk, Herman Hammond, and his wife, Melba Dixon, in these letters to Lila Rose Parker. I really think the murderer had to be one of those three. Why else would he write about them so much? Perhaps he was trying to sort out his thoughts about all of them." Nicole paused, suddenly feeling excited. "Or he suspected one of them would try to kill him and so he tried to communicate in code, in a way, with Lila Rose Parker! Maybe one of them murdered him, or even worse, maybe all of them were in on it!" Suddenly, the ladies heard a strange banging sound coming from the second floor below them.

"Ghosts!" Lia said before laughing.

"Now don't go putting any ideas in my head, Lia! Bad enough that I can't sleep in my own house tonight, let alone the fact that this house isn't even completely renovated yet. All this creaking is getting to me. I really hope this place isn't haunted!" said Nicole.

"Come on, silly! Besides, that would be bad for business. Let's head downstairs to the second floor and pick two adjoining guest rooms. At least most of the bedrooms are in good order now, plus I know we already stocked up on additional pajamas, in case any guests ever need them. I guess we're going to have to break them in!" said Lia, with a huge grin on her face.

"You seem way too excited about this sleep-over!" said Nicole, shaking her head. As they traveled down one flight of stairs, Nicole couldn't stop thinking about the three possible suspects who could have killed the owner of that home. And then it suddenly occurred to her: Jack Dixon was murdered in this house! Why had she never really considered that before? And in which room did the murder take place?

Nicole tried to recall the information she had come across in the past, whether from the historical society or in old news pieces often re-featured in the *Rosewood Gazette*. She knew the articles had identified that he was discovered unconscious on the floor in his study. But which room was that? They all looked the same to her. Each beautiful room had a gorgeous fireplace, along with very ornate walls and wooden floors. How could she know? She shook her head, deciding that it should not matter. It was probably better if she did not know. A bit shaken, she followed Lia's lead down the hall as she went into several rooms, inspecting them for feasibility for their stay-over. Eventually, Lia emerged and said, "Let's take these two rooms! They both seem to have a little bit more light reflecting off the river, despite the storm. And this way we're next to each other!" She had grabbed some pajamas that she had found in one of the closets and handed a pair to Nicole. "Here you go. The bathroom attached to your room has soap, toothpaste, toothbrushes, and anything you might need. Okay?" said Lia.

In a daze, Nicole accepted the pajamas and hugged her friend good night. She dizzily went into the room designated for her and closed the door. Despite having lived in Texas for one of her chemical engineering jobs years ago, she was not one for living away from home. She had even traveled a lot, many times around the world, and yet she could never get used to the idea of being away from her own bed. The irony and funny part this time was, she was the true owner of this house! And yet she felt like a total stranger that evening. Perhaps it was the power failure, or perhaps it was the newfound knowledge about this strange Lila Rose Parker and what her letters may hold in terms of new information, but she could not seem to shake an eerie feeling that hung over her.

Nicole focused on trying to get dressed and ready for bed. After freshening up and changing her clothes, all by flashlight, she got into bed and tried to get settled. She thought about how lucky they were that the house was renovated as much as it has been. What if they'd gotten stuck in the house when none of the rooms were ready?

Exhausted and tired, she struggled to keep her eyes open despite the strangeness of the room and being away from her home, until she suddenly thought about Ringo. She panicked momentarily, worried about him. Thankfully, she had left water and food in the kitchen before she had gone to the cafe earlier that day, so her nerves dissipated quite quickly. And then she also remembered that he'd be okay because of the doggie door. He could get himself outside when needed (of course, she hoped he wouldn't do that during the storm, though). Nicole resolved in her mind that she would go back for him in the morning when it was safe to travel on the roads again. Once her plan was set, she let herself drift off to sleep, thinking warmly of her beloved black labrador retriever at first.

As Nicole fell more deeply asleep, however, she had many strange dreams about the Cannoli Cafe, Neelam, and Dean. She tossed and turned for what felt like an hour until she was suddenly tapped on the shoulder to wake up. Before opening her eyes, she assumed it was Lia. "Lia! What is it now? I was finally asleep!" she groaned.

Strangely, Nicole did not hear an answer. Confused, she opened her eyes and then gasped. Staring back at her was the translucent face of none other than Jack Dixon!

CHAPTER FIVE

NICOLE STARED AHEAD IN DISBELIEF. Was this a dream? She quickly pinched her forearm and felt pain. Unable to breathe, she stared up at the face peering at her as its "body" floated above her. Translucent and illuminated, the figure above her was absolutely that of Jack Dixon. She recalled the way he looked from the photos she had seen in the attic. Slightly balding, with a dark mustache and a stocky figure, Jack Dixon was hanging above her fourposter bed.

"Hello, Nicole! I think you know who I am, and that I need your help. I've been trapped in this house for 100 years, and I cannot move on to the afterlife until you help solve the mystery of who murdered me. I just have not been able to move on because I don't know the answer to that question."

Nicole suddenly interrupted Jack Dixon. "Wait, wait, wait! Is this a dream? This can't be real, right?" Feeling awkward lying in bed, she pushed herself up and rested against the headboard. Jack mirrored her, floating down to "stand" beside the bed, near her.

"I would suggest you view this however you need to view it, whether it is a dream or as a ghostly visit in real life. It does not matter. All you need to know is that you have to solve this mystery. I need you to help me solve it so I can move on." Despite his translucent nature, his eyes seemed to burn into hers. He was serious. And for not having a proper body, his voice was very deep. Being the engineer she was, Nicole wondered how that was possible.

Nicole took in a deep breath and noticed the faint smell of tobacco, in the room. Did aromas from the 1920s also accompany this apparition? Perhaps Jack Dixon smoked a lot. This was all too surreal for her. She winced, feeling overwhelmed, and decided to view the experience as a dream. It was a little less scary that way. Suddenly, she noticed Jack float across the room; he grabbed a robe off the coat rack in the corner by the door. "Here,

Nicole. Put this on so we can go downstairs and you can view a scene of one of my last memories in this house. He nodded to her and held the robe up to her. A gentleman, he continued to hold the robe so she could place her arms inside. Now being inches away from him, she struggled to keep her composure together. She really wanted to run away from the entire experience, but since the pinch earlier did not seem to do anything as it did not wake her up to her real life, she assumed she was stuck in the dream until Jack Dixon felt he was done with her.

Nicole tied the velvet robe closed and then turned around to find him opening the door for her to exit the room. "What about Lia?" she asked.

"No, Nicole. This time, you need to do this on your own with me. Now, we don't have much time. Let's go!" Time? What did he know about time? She wondered. She wasn't even sure what this was!

Jack Dixon floated down the hallway and occasionally looked back to make sure she was still following him. She followed along slowly, attempting to compute everything she was seeing. Why did everything paradoxically look the same, but not? The house bore a distinct interior design to Nicole, not the way they had renovated it. She could see the wallpaper was different in the hallways, and everything seemed a bit fresher. As she gripped the handle of the railing to go down the stairs, she realized the stairs seemed quite new and unlike the worn appearance from when they purchased the house. A chill went down her spine. She was not only with the 1920s ghost of Jack Dixon, but the entire house was back in the 1920s! Nicole wondered about the mechanics of what she was experiencing. Where was Lia? Back in the real world? Perhaps her sleeping body was not even in this 1920s house, which disappointed Nicole. She would have had more peace of mind if she knew there was a chance Lia could appear somehow, despite what Jack Dixon said. At the same time, however, she did not want her friend to experience the stress she was currently under.

As she traveled down the stairs, she gripped the railing firmly and admired the wood-paneled walls as she descended. *Gorgeous*, she thought to herself, as it was not the mid-century wood paneling people are familiar with today; this was ornately carved wood paneling from the Victorian era. Amazed, she continued to follow her ghostly companion as he made his way through the downstairs and into the kitchen. Then, she noticed he moved the back wall in the kitchen and revealed a doorway!

"Come, Nicole. There is something you need to see." She watched as the ghostly Jack Dixon opened the door that led to a dark staircase below. Again, his illuminated figure showed her the way. As she looked around the kitchen, prior to going down the stairs, she felt like she was in a historical house museum given the softwood preparation table, wood flooring, cupboards, and an old stove design. She had to remind herself she was in a dream, or at least that's what she kept telling herself.

Nicole continued down the stairs and followed Jack Dixon as he made his way into what appeared to be a small distillery. Given her chemical engineering career, she immediately recognized what was in front of her: a moonshine operation! Nicole suddenly felt very shaken as she realized Jack Dixon was revealing a major clue to her. His death most likely had something to do with this operation. While she did not have many history or English courses as an engineering major in college, there was one thing she distinctly recalled from her high school history classes: Prohibition. And Prohibition would have rendered this operation illegal in the 1920s. But back then, people relied on the illegal trade of alcohol, and of course, manufacture (such as moonshine) so that they could still consume.

Interestingly, the consumption itself was not illegal, from what she recalled, but the trade, transportation, and manufacture of alcoholic beverages were illegal.

Fascinated by the setup, she hid in a corner as she inspected their operation. She also noticed a few other men working in that secret basement, bottling the moonshine at the end of the process, then placing the bottles into small crates. She wondered how they managed the transportation aspect of the trade, whether there was "bootlegging" (bottles in boots) involved, or if Jack Dixon and his people somehow managed a more sophisticated transfer with other traders and customers. Given Jack's prominence and control of the town, she suspected the latter.

Nicole's mind raced as she tried to piece together as much as she could about the scene in front of her, recognizing what Jack said about the time constraint (even if she did not understand it). Jack. Where was Jack? Nicole suddenly realized she could not see the ghost of Jack Dixon anymore, but instead saw Jack Dixon as he appeared in person in the early 1920s, standing in front of Frederick Clemmons!

"Now listen here, Jack Dixon! I've invested my

lifetime savings in this operation, and I don't like what I'm seeing. We're not making enough profit! You have to stop feeling bad for people who don't have enough money. Charge more! Charge more! We are putting our reputations on the line for this, and you decide not to be a shrewd businessman now?" said Frederick Clemmons, Jack's business partner.

Jack Dixon slammed his hand on the table nearest them. "Freddie! We're charging them an arm and a leg, as it is! And if we don't keep our prices lower than the competition, we won't get any business! Everybody's got these operations going. The only way to recoup your investment in all of this, especially given how we've secured the supplies and materials in advance, is we have to keep doing what we're doing. Otherwise, you lose all of your investment!" yelled Jack Dixon, spittle spewing out of his mouth as he argued with his business partner.

"Look, Jack. While this operation may be in your basement, you know that via this tunnel, I can access all this from my house and property that sits behind yours," said Frederick Clemmons, gesturing to a door in the wall. "I'm prepared to remove everything and put it in my basement. It's smaller than yours, but it can do the job. And no one but

Melba knows that you have this down here. We've got the guys entering your basement from my property right now. It wouldn't take much for me to reconstruct my basement, set up operations there, and take all this away from you! Not to mention the fact that we've already lost business on your Dixon's Goods and Wares shop in the past, and I bailed you out that time, too! You are a bad business person, Jack Dixon. It needs to end, and you need to give me full control. I've had enough!" screamed Frederick Clemmons.

Nicole, shaking, took in a deep breath — completely in shock that she was witnessing a critical conversation in the history of Waterford, New Jersey. And she could not believe that Jack Dixon, the religious resident, whom everybody loved in the 1920s, had an illegal operation going on beneath the very house she purchased a hundred years later. Unbelievable.

Suddenly, the room began to spin, and her heart raced. And before she knew it, she was asleep again in her bed in the 2020s.

CHAPTER SIX

NICOLE, with beads of perspiration hugging her hairline, woke up to the sound of music downstairs in her Victorian bed-and-breakfast. This time, however, she did not see the translucent Jack Dixon, but she sensed she was still under his purview, especially since the music sounded like it was from the 1920s. She eyed the robe on the coat rack again in the corner and decided she was best off to wander through the house and explore what was going on. If she could figure out who truly murdered Jack Dixon, perhaps she could escape these nightmares, and if he was stuck in some sort of purgatory, per se, he would finally be freed. She shook her head, not sure she really believed all that, but she knew one thing for sure: she wanted to go back to her old life, and solving this murder was the only way to move forward!

After pulling the robe over her shoulder, she exited her bedroom and headed down the stairs once again. She felt the smooth railing again beneath her fingers, the music becoming louder and louder as she approached the first floor. Once she arrived, she was bedazzled with the sight before her: men wearing tuxedos and women dressed in beautiful gowns, with martinis being carried on trays by bartenders and servers — not to mention an assortment of food throughout the house. She walked among the guests, but they did not seem to notice her. In the last dream, she wasn't sure if they could see her in the basement, so she had hid in the corner to watch the argument. Now, at least she knew for sure she was not visible. She chuckled to herself as she considered the idea she was experiencing time travel. All in all, this was a crazy experience and one that she never expected when she left the Cannoli Cafe less than twenty-four hours before.

Nicole, wondering if she was again against some sort of time constraint as Jack hinted at in the first experience, picked up her pace as she inspected the first level rooms very quickly for clues. She visited the parlor and the kitchen, but she could not find Jack Dixon anywhere. Unsure of what she should be looking for, she continued to check the faces of all the guests as they were partying, dancing, and talking. Perhaps the murderer was at this very party? She suddenly felt panic stricken, concerned that perhaps she was on the wrong path to assume it was one of the three individuals Jack wrote about it in his letters. Perhaps it was someone else entirely!

Just as she started to wind herself up, she spotted the translucent Jack Dixon floating across the room. Relieved, she approached him. He winked at her as she neared him and moved his head quickly, in a gesture to suggest she should exit through the front door and go to the front porch. And then he faded away. *Interesting*, she thought. It had not occurred to her to check the outside. When she exited the front door, she was shocked to see the surrounding Victorian homes on the outside, as it looks quite different than in the 2020s; the vicinity had obviously been redeveloped in Nicole's lifetime now that she could see what it looked like in the past. As she walked on the wraparound porch, she eventually found the 1920s Jack Dixon and his wife, Melba, arguing profusely.

"Jack! I don't know how you could do this to our family! Why did you ever agree on starting that moonshine business with Frederick Clemmons?" yelled Melba.

"Shh! Melba! Be quiet. Come on, you're going to blow our cover! And you know why. I owe Frederick big time. He wanted to start this business, he wanted to invest in it, and he wanted me to be his partner so that he didn't have to put up all the money! I owed him for all of his help getting us out of our bind years ago at the Goods and Wares store." He paused, catching his breath. "Melba, things are getting out of control, and I don't need any trouble from you at the moment." Jack started pacing in front of his wife, upset. All of a sudden, his mustached round face grew quite red, and he slammed his fist into the side of the house. "Melba, I've had just about enough from you. I just do not need any more problems. Just worry about our son, Robert, and leave everything else to me. Understand?"

Nicole watched as Melba's face grew very tight. Her eyes went into a slit, and she clenched her teeth. Speaking between her teeth, she said, "You are going to regret this, Jack Dixon. Mark my words. I will not have you corrupt our Robert by having this business. If only Frederick would go off and do the business himself. Do whatever you have to do to get out of it. Do you understand? Or I will take matters into my own hands."

"Yeah? What are you going to do?" said Jack in a very mocking tone.

"That Raymond Ackerman, the guy always hanging around your store and our property, already threatened to bring all this out to the papers!" Melba said, her face now equally as red as Jack's — in the moonlight and surrounded by lanterns. "What if things get out of hand with him? I'm fearing for our safety! He's been demanding money to keep him quiet. And he's becoming more aggressive!"

"That guy is a joke. Don't worry about him. And no one will believe him. I'm headed to get a drink. I suggest you do the same," said Jack.

"So you walk away and do not feel concerned about our family's safety? How dare you!" she screamed. Jack waved his hand in the air and just kept walking.

As Nicole watched Jack Dixon saunter off, and Melba trail behind — tears streaming down her face with clenched teeth — Nicole wondered about the identity of the murderer. Was it Frederick? Or could it possibly be Melba? Or did something go awry, and the murderer was really this Raymond Ackerman she spoke of? And if it were Melba, would she really do that to her family — her son? *Although, when people fear for their safety, they can go pretty far*, she thought. Especially in her experience, particularly after being held up at gunpoint a few times!

Somehow, she knew she still did not have all the information she needed. There was still the third name she had found in the letters, that of Herman Hammond. And then she suddenly realized she was probably onto another dream after this one. Just as she had that thought, the whole earth spun, and she was suddenly back in her bed upstairs, once again.

CHAPTER SEVEN

NICOLE OPENED HER EYES, wondering if she was finally waking up in the real world or in yet another dream. Jack Dixon's dream, that is. Or in the past. She shook her head, not really knowing what was going on. At the same time, however, she knew she had to persevere — to figure out who really killed Jack Dixon. Just then, translucent Jack entered the room from the door and said, "Come, Nicole. Let me take you to my store, Dixon's Goods and Wares. There is something you need to see." The translucent Jack Dixon took her hand, guided her to the coat rack, and held the robe for her once again. After nodding to her, he guided her out of the room and the next thing she knew, she was outside what appeared to be a 1920s general store in the town of

Rosewood, New Jersey. She cautiously opened the door. Inside, she found Herman Hammond, the store clerk who worked for Jack. Since it appeared to be dark outside, she surmised it was the end of the day, where Herman was wrapping up and counting all the bills while making notations in a book. There was a finely dressed woman in front of Herman at the counter.

Herman slammed his pencil down. "Well, I'm just so angry, Margaret! If I knew that Jack Dixon was involved in all this moonshine, and bringing in the money, I could have been profiting, as well!" Herman slammed his fist down on the counter next to the cash register.

Margaret shook her head. "But Herman! I would not have wanted you involved in that. I'm okay with the modest lifestyle. I don't know why you're so bent on living it up and moving your station up in life!" Margaret touched Herman's arm across the counter, but he violently backed away and started pacing, clearly agitated. Nicole stood still, watching as the heavily mustached man stewed. She suddenly felt a chill. While she mentally knew they could not see her, she still felt exposed somehow — how awkward it was to witness this private argument, just as it was uncomfortable to see the other two arguments in the previous dreams. Nicole considered how odd, yet insightful, it was to watch these scenes from the 1920s. She looked around and did not see where the ghostly Jack Dixon was. In fact, she did not recall ever seeing him in the store once he led her there. But it did not matter. She knew what she had to do.

While Herman paced, and Margaret looked on with tears streaming down her face, Nicole took a moment to examine all the unique items in his store. She found it quite interesting, the idea of everyone in town coming to his store to do their general orders. He appeared to have textiles, and a wide range of things that anyone could purchase — from canned food to newspapers to sewing kits, and even children's toys. She concluded that this was probably the only way to get anything ordered in that you might need. Otherwise, how could you find anything?

No wonder Jack was at the heart of the trade operations for moonshine during the Prohibition era. And despite what Frederick said in the other dream, he probably knew he needed to partner with Jack because of his reputation and connections. Jack probably knew everybody in the trade business, who he could trust and who he could not. You don't become that popular if you don't have a good network.

Nicole reflected on the first dream and wondered what exactly went wrong in the operations piece of the business that it was not profitable enough. After recalling Jack's remarks, she surmised that perhaps it was simply too much competition, after all; Jack most likely wanted to get a leg up initially by being everybody's number one supplier. Maybe that's what worked for him in the past with the general store, if there had been another one he was competing with — in a nearby town, perhaps. He was probably pretty business savvy, knowing his friends could invest and help on a short-term basis. The key was to hook the customers and get them devoted from the get-go. In terms of the moonshine, chances were he planned to raise the prices once he hooked his customers on the trade operation by showing he could deliver, especially given the complexity (and illegality). That was a decent business model and would've made sense, except it seemed that his business partner, Frederick Clemmons, grew impatient. Now, it appeared that Nicole was witnessing the fact that Herman Hammond was not in on the entire operation, feeling very left out and extremely angry about it. The whole story fascinated Nicole, since the moonshine piece was completely left out of the letters. And yet Jack must have suspected back then that he was a target by one of those three individuals, the people he wrote Lila Rose Parker about!

Suddenly, Herman stopped pacing and raised his fists in the air. "I could just kill that Jack Dixon! In fact, I punched his lights out the other day. Just wish I had finished the job!" Herman then slammed both fists down on the countertop, making Margaret jump back. "Do you know how much I've done for that guy in this store? I run this whole place! And he and Frederick just sit back collecting the money. Unbelievable! He leaves me out of it?" Herman was *furious*, that much was clear to Nicole. When she looked at the expression on Margaret's face, she could see how surprised and upset she was to see Herman that way.

Nicole's body began to feel very heavy. She noticed the rooms started to spin, and she was thrust back into her bed, for which she hoped was the last time. Half-asleep and half awake, she considered everything that had been presented before her. There were three major suspects: Frederick Clemmons, Melba Dixon, and Herman Hammond. And a fourth possibly — Raymond

Ackerman, who was threatening Melba and the family, but Nicole felt he was a less likely suspect since Jack did not mention him; she figured out that Jack had good instincts and trusted them. How funny to trust the instincts of someone who was technically dead!

As she considered all the possibilities, she realized they all had something in common: gripes about the moonshine operation, whether they were left out or whether they objected to it, or whether they thought they could perform even better. Somehow, Nicole had to figure out which of these individuals had enough motive or reason to take Jack's life. Who would have been angry enough to kill the prominent Jack Dixon? Now that was the question!

CHAPTER EIGHT

NICOLE, her eyes still closed, was startled to hear birds chirping outside her window. *Could it be,* she thought. Did she finally emerge from that string of dreams, of ghostly appearances? She reflected on the strange night she had while staying in her newly purchased Victorian home. She shuddered to think of what might have happened had guests stayed here before her, although she had always planned on doing a test night, so to speak. Was it truly haunted? Perhaps her subconscious was simply working on all the information that had been presented to her — from old articles and the letters she and Lia had found. She recalled seeing articles about the mystery of Jack Dixon on occasion in the Rosewood Gazette.

As Nicole stretched her body in the bed, she continued to ponder the strange experience from the previous eight hours. She was not sure exactly what she had been through the previous night, but she was certain of one thing: she still had to figure out who murdered Jack Dixon. Taking in a deep breath, she opened her eyes and looked around the room. Given the storm and power failure, she was unable to admire the very room she was staying in the previous night. Beautifully adorned with textured wallpaper, a fireplace that was nearly magical, and with the bright sun shining through the sparkling windows, she felt quite pleased at how much progress they had made in terms of the renovations. Suddenly, the door opened.

"Good morning, sleepyhead!" said Lia, bearing a breakfast tray in hand. "I heard you groaning all night! Nightmares? I figured you could use breakfast in bed. Here, I've got toast, eggs, and coffee." Lia approached the bed with the tray, and Nicole sat more upright against the headboard.

"Lia, you don't know the half of it. I had what might have been the best or worst night of my life, depending on how you look at it." Nicole accepted the tray and promptly stirred the creamer in her coffee, feeling very fatigued from the night before. She hoped that the coffee would revive her.

"What? What do you mean, best or worst night or your life?" Lia furrowed her eyebrows.

"I'm not sure if this place is haunted, or if I simply had a series of bad dreams. All I know is that I was somehow transported in time, and I witnessed Jack Dixon and his business partners, in addition to his wife, in this house and in his store during the 1920s."

Lia put her hand up to Nicole's forehead. "Are you feeling okay? Should you go to the doctor?" asked Lia.

"I'm fine, Lia. But I'm serious about last night. I think what I saw in these dreams or visions or what-ever they were, is critical to us solving this mystery. And I suspect we will not have peace in this house until we resolve who truly killed Jack Dixon." Nicole lifted the coffee cup to her lips, savoring the hot and delicious coffee. That was one good thing about owning both businesses; she could ensure the coffee at the bed-and-breakfast was on point!

"So, how do you want to proceed? Do you want to tell me everything now, or should we tell the whole town and get all their heads together on this one?" Lia paused. "Especially considering the town history. We may need more information!" Lia's face brightened in excitement.

Nicole took another sip of the steaming hot coffee, grateful for the warmth of the cup in her hands and the beverage on her lips. She still felt so shaken to the bone, given her experience the night before. "I think that's a good idea, Lia. Let's get the whole town in on this one. I suspect the Knitting for Good ladies probably have some information we can use. But is it safe to travel on the road? And, quite frankly, I want to go home first to change and freshen up. Plus, I want to check on Ringo before we go to the cafe."

"Slow down, slow down! Vince Mongelli called the desk downstairs earlier! I forgot to tell you. Wait till you hear this! He's coming over with Aunt Lucia in a giant Hummer; he got it from one of his buddies. The roads still have some water, but he said we should be okay if we travel in the Hummer back to Rosewood."

Nicole laughed. Vince Mongelli was a reformed gangster who was now her Aunt Lucia's dear friend and companion. She felt quite grateful to him, especially because he helped save her life in the last case. She was glad he was now fully recovered from his injuries, to the point where he could drive around in the Hummer! It would also comfort her to see her Aunt Lucia, so she was happy to hear the plans from Lia. "It all sounds wonderful! Maybe he can drive us back to my house, and then we can freshen up and head over to the cafe."

Nicole promptly changed her clothes and got ready to be rescued by Vince Mongelli and her Aunt Lucia. She marveled at how there was never a dull moment in Rosewood!

"So let me get this straight, Nicole!" said Tommy, their contractor. "You want me to destroy the back wall of the kitchen to see if there is some sort of secret basement?" Tommy, with his rough skin and large build, nearly intimidated Nicole with his question. Nicole, Lia, Tommy, Aunt Lucia, and Vince Mongelli were all standing in the kitchen at the Victorian house. Tommy had visited to check on the ladies, suspecting they probably got trapped there. And he still had work to do on the house, of course, in terms of the renovations.

"It could be a usable space, so we ought to find that out now before we open up the bed-and-break-fast. Besides, we already have the second floor done, and pretty soon you'll be done with the third floor where you found that secret room. By the way, I figured you can simply fix up the third floor and we can use that for storage," said Nicole.

Aunt Lucia looked over to Nicole with soft, old eyes. "What is it, Nicole? Why do you think something is down there?" asked Aunt Lucia. Aunt Lucia clearly knew Nicole well enough to realize that something was up. "Do you think there's something about Jack Dixon's murder down there?" Everyone in the kitchen gasped.

Tommy grunted, "Ha. You know what's funny? That would make sense about a second basement. Because the current basement, which we enter from the outside, does not really cover the entire first floor. It would make sense that there could be another room down there, possibly." He paused, looking at all the surprised faces. Nicole realized they were still probably getting over the idea of possibly finding another clue about the murder in a secret room. "Well, it's gonna cost you!" said Tommy. Lia and Nicole laughed.

"I could have told you that!" said Lia. Everyone chuckled, knowing how good Lia was with numbers. "Well, if we do find a space down there, maybe we can find a use for it. Perhaps some sort of activity room, or game room for the guests."

"That's a great idea! I personally think you should put a pool table down there," everyone chuckled again, knowing Vince Mongelli's background. For some reason, everyone equates pool with gangsters.

"Okay, ladies. So I'll have my guys figure out what to do with this wall and find a way to get to this secret room you think is down there. I'm just warning you, though, if there is no secret room we'll have to repair the wall and it was all for a lost cause." He made a funny face.

"Not a problem, Tommy. Now, what did you say earlier about driving Lia's car over?" asked Nicole.

"Oh yeah, compliments of the house! Vince can take you ladies over to Nicole's house, and I'll drive Lia's car over to the cafe later today with my guys. How about a few free coffees and cannolis?" Tommy winked.

Nicole laughed. "Now that's a deal we can't pass up!" Lia nodded vigorously in agreement.

CHAPTER NINE

BARK, bark, bark!

"Thanks for waiting, Aunt Lucia and Vince. I feel so refreshed now with a new set of clothes and a shower!" said Nicole as she rubbed Ringo's back. She had put on a fresh blouse and capris since it was summer. Ringo was clearly happy that his owner had returned, wagging his tail and jumping around the house. They were sitting in Nicole's living room as they waited for Lia to finish her turn in the shower. It had gotten to the point where Lia stayed over so often, Lia actually had extra sets of clothes and other items in Nicole's home. They had even debated on moving in together at one point, but Lia decided she would still like to keep her home for the time being, as long as everything worked out with their new bed-and-breakfast together. Plus, with the uncertainty of Nicole's future with Dean, they decided it was best not to make any changes.

"It's our pleasure. We're just glad that you ladies are safe, especially since you got stuck in Waterford overnight with all the flooding, downed lines, and treacherous conditions. Have you spoken with your mom, dad, or Stephen?" asked Aunt Lucia. Nicole's parents had a second home in Texas, where they often stayed for parts of the year. Her brother, Stephen, also an engineer, lived and worked in Texas.

"Not since the storm, no. Why? Are they worried?" asked Nicole. Nicole pulled her fingers through her moist hair, relishing how clean it felt. Somehow, she needed to wash away the eeriness of the night before!

"I texted your mother this morning. I told her our plans to rescue you, so your parents wouldn't worry. Apparently, there were some news reports about how bad the storm was in New Jersey. Some other areas of the state were much worse off!" said Aunt Lucia.

Nicole was amused to hear her aunt say she "texted" anyone. She then glanced over her shoulder to see Vince on his way outside the kitchen door with Ringo for fresh air.

Lia came down the hallway and into the living room. "Oh, I'm so exhausted. I just feel like using Nicole's streaming service and lounging around all day!" Aunt Lucia and Nicole laughed.

"Since when are you lazy?" asked Nicole. Generally, both ladies were very hard-working, but of course, they relished the occasional chance to sit back, enjoy a glass of wine paired with cheese, and stream a show or two.

"Not often, since you're constantly fueling me up with coffees and cappuccinos! By the way, I sent a text message to Neelam to meet us at the cafe. Is that okay?" asked Lia. Both Aunt Lucia and Nicole furrowed their eyebrows quizzically as they listened to Lia.

"So much texting going on in this house!" Nicole laughed. "Of course, why would it not be okay?" she asked.

"Well, I just want to make sure you were okay with it because, in the more recent past, it's been you and me solving mysteries together. But perhaps Neelam might have a unique perspective this time. I think we need all the help we can get on this one!

Besides, she was part of our mystery club when we were kids, remember?"

Aunt Lucia laughed. "I always got a kick out of you girls solving those little kid mysteries way back when. Like what happened to Mrs. Sandberg's newspaper? Or who stole Johnny's skateboard?" All three ladies laughed.

Vince then came back into the house with Ringo and suggested that they get going. After they piled into his borrowed Hummer, and made it across town, Nicole was shocked to see the cafe nearly full, as if they were all awaiting their arrival. As soon as they walked in, the entire cafe reacted with applause.

"Well! Apparently, we're celebrities now in town!" said Lia. "We need to get trapped in that house more often!" Nicole jabbed her friend lightly in the elbow.

"Ladies, please sit down. We've been waiting anxiously for you!" urged Doris, one of the Knitting for Good ladies. Charlotte and Mary looked on, nodding and smiling. Something was definitely up, Nicole surmised.

"Please go ahead," Nicole said to Lia, Aunt Lucia, and Vince. "Let me just check with Susie for a second in the back." As Nicole headed towards the kitchen, Susie met her halfway behind the counter.

Susie gave Nicole a warm hug. "Oh, I'm just so happy you are okay, Nicole!"

"Susie? What's going on?" asked Nicole, squinting her eyes and smiling, curious to see what Susie would say.

"Well, there was the matter of Tommy calling his mom, Charlotte!" answered Susie.

"Aha! That explains it!" Nicole raised her finger in the air. "He must have told Charlotte that I think there's a secret room in the basement! No wonder the whole town is here. Once one of those Knitting for Good ladies gets wind of anything, word travels fast." Susie and Nicole chuckled together. "Well, I'd better get back to the table. Wait till everyone hears what I have to say!" said Nicole.

"Cappuccinos and cannolis for everyone?" asked Susie.

"Of course!" Nicole grinned. As she made her way back to the table, she admired the view of all her dear friends. Don Martini and Max were at the table, as well as Aunt Lucia and Vince Mongelli, in addition to the Knitting for Good ladies, and Lia (of course). Then, suddenly, everyone turned around. Nicole shifted her gaze, as well, to find Neelam walking in with a surprise. Beth!

Neelam approached Nicole and gave her a big hug. "Good morning! Now, what did I tell you? I *knew* you were going to come across another mystery, didn't I?" said Neelam. Beth stood quietly beside her, listening with her head cocked.

"You're always right, Neelam. You're always right." Nicole laughed and then turned to Beth. "Good morning, Beth. Can I get you anything? Thank you for joining us."

Nicole's brown eyes met Beth's blue eyes; there was always an intensity about Beth's eyes that fascinated Nicole. Beth carefully and slowly replied, "Good morning. I'm glad you and Lia are okay. I heard you got trapped at your new house in Waterford. That house is so interesting, isn't it?" remarked Beth.

Nicole was intrigued that Beth commented on her experience. Curious about Beth's remark, she replied, "Oh? I didn't know you followed what was going on in town?"

Neelam suddenly chimed in. "I was checking out the space next to Beth's store to prepare for our toy business, and I told Beth what happened. I suggested that she come here this morning." Beth nodded in agreement as Neelam explained how she had arrived and discovered the events of the previous day.

"Well, you're certainly welcome, Beth. I'm glad you're here. Truly. Please go ahead and sit at that large table that they all put together. Looks like we have a lot of sleuthing to do!" said Nicole.

CHAPTER TEN

As THE SUN shone through the large windows into the Cannoli Cafe, Nicole took in the scene before her. It was so comforting to see all of her friends gathered around her at the enormous table assembled by her friends. The cafe was certainly abuzz, with everyone gossiping about Nicole and Lia being trapped at the house the previous night, talk of Jack Dixon and anything they could recall about him, and a possible secret basement!

"Now hush, everyone! We need to give the professor the floor!" said Mr. Don Martini. Don often referred to Nicole as the professor, and she now winced at that reference. It suddenly conjured up visions of her former students, not to mention the phone call she had received the previous day from her friend Gabriel, head of Information Technology at the University of New Jersey. Fortunately, the frightening night had a silver lining: she had nearly forgotten about the job opportunity at the university. Dr. Nicole Capula, Professor of Practice? Sensing the pit in her stomach, she decided she needed to park that train of thought. For the time being, at least. She needed to focus on the issue at hand — Jack Dixon's murder.

"Thank you, Mr. Martini! Now, I need to preface what I am about to tell you." She paused, all eyes on her. "I don't really know if what I experienced was real or not real. Perhaps they were simply dreams, or nightmares, depending on how you look at it. I don't even think it really matters. But I do think that the experiences I had in the 1920s were very insightful." Nicole looked around and saw several blank faces.

"Look, dear. I think you need to back up and start over. What happened when you arrived in the rain yesterday at your house in Waterford?" asked Max in his soft, gentle voice.

Nicole cringed. She realized she was still so stressed and preoccupied with the reminder of her university life, that she wasn't very composed in getting back to her sleuthing life — to properly explain what had happened at the house last night. She inhaled slowly and tried to get herself together. "Right. So, we arrived at the house. And as Tommy left, he told us to walk up to the third floor and go through the hole in the wall to find a secret room in the attic. There, Lia and I had found old items such as candlesticks, along with photos of Jack Dixon's business partners and family. I had recognized the figures from the historical society presentations we've seen in the past here in town. Oh, and there were chests with old letters inside them."

"Wow! Now, this is getting exciting!" said Mary with a wide grin. "Were these romantic letters?" she asked, shaking her shoulders a bit in delight. Everyone chuckled.

"Well, perhaps they had a childhood affinity for one another. That part isn't clear. But the letters were exchanged between Jack Dixon and a Lila Rose Parker." At this point, Nicole paused and looked around the room. She was surprised to see that Beth was rubbing her chin with her hand, and was listening intently as Nicole spoke. Nicole continued. "It seems that Lila Rose Parker was a friend, and Jack Dixon had written profusely about his business partner, Frederick Clemmons; his clerk, Herman Hammond; and, of course his wife, Melba Dixon. Now, the interesting thing is each of the dreams, or ghostly apparitions I experienced, featured the three people mentioned in these letters." Everyone gasped.

"Wait, you saw a ghost? Your bed-and-breakfast is haunted?" asked Charlotte.

Nicole shook her head. "Again, perhaps they were simply dreams that I had. In fact, I believe they were, because the dreams showed the house in the 1920s, and it actually looked a lot different from how it appears today. And the critical detail I saw was this: a secret distillery in the basement of the house!"

Everyone gasped. "A distillery, you said?" asked Don Martini. "What were they producing in a basement?"

"Yes. A distillery. Apparently, Jack Dixon had a secret business producing moonshine during the Prohibition era with his business partner, Frederick Clemmons!" Everyone's jaws dropped. "On top of that, Melba Dixon was very unhappy about it. I witnessed an altercation between them in the second dream. And in the third dream, I saw that Herman Hammond, his store clerk, was furious that he was not included in the moonshine business. He thought he was missing out."

The entire room was silent.

Lia piped up. "Anything else you think we should know, Nicole?"

"I got the impression Frederick Clemmons invested a significant portion, actually all of his life savings rather, into the business." Nicole paused as everyone digested all the information.

Vince Mongelli put his cannoli down and spoke up. "Sounds to me like he was murdered due to this moonshine business. One, or all three of them, did him in!" Everyone else nodded in agreement.

"I agree, Nicole. Well, I do think your dreams are insightful, and now we need to figure out the next steps. Do any of you know anything more about the history of Jack Dixon and his family?" asked Lia.

"It sounds to me, dear, that you know most of the history from the historical society presentations in the past. That's probably what helped you iden-tify who was who in the dreams, or anything you found in the attic. But maybe you should go visit with Christina Morano, in the library, and see what she can dig up on the archives," said Doris, one of the Knitting for Good ladies.

Beth shocked everyone by chiming in. "That sounds like a good idea. I think your best bet is to go to the library next. That's very logical. When do you think you might go?" she asked.

Nicole was surprised by Beth's interest. Did she want to join them at the library? "Well, I need to meet the Sorria sisters, my cousins, about the bed-and-breakfast later today. But Lia and I will probably go to the library tomorrow. Would you like to join us, Beth? Neelam, what about you?"

Neelam and Beth both nodded and said yes in unison.

Aunt Lucia said, "You ladies are certainly getting the mystery club together. Plus, now you've got a new member!" Everyone laughed.

"Sounds like a brilliant plan. See you all at 10 AM tomorrow. I'll text Christina to let her know what we're looking for in advance," said Nicole. With a firm plan in place, everyone smiled and passed around the tray of cannolis. Nicole was happy that they had decided on the next steps to solve the most famous murder in town. Even though she didn't get many suggestions during her town meeting, so to speak, she was glad she had shared what happened, just in case anyone might later have a lightbulb moment or make a connection she hadn't previously considered.

And, though she experienced her dreams alone the night before, she was thrilled to be in good company now.

CHAPTER ELEVEN

As PROMISED, Lia's car was waiting for her in the back parking lot behind the Cannoli Cafe. "Thank goodness for Tommy!" said Lia as she buckled into the driver's seat. After their sleuthing session with the entire town, or what felt like the entire town of Rosewood, Lia and Nicole were heading back to the Victorian house; Maria and Amy Sorria, Nicole's cousins, were arriving in Waterford that afternoon to check out the house and talk about their new upcoming roles as managers for the bed-and-breakfast. "By the way, Nicole, how come I'm always driving?" asked Lia, glancing over at her friend.

"You are a buster, Lia! I don't know. Look at my hatchback. Do you want me to drive us over in *that*? Or do you want to drive in style?" answered Nicole as they exited the back parking lot behind the Cannoli Cafe.

"Ha! Guess you have a point, my friend. Okay, then!" remarked Lia.

As Lia and Nicole headed out of town into Waterford, Nicole peered out the window to inspect the damage on the roads from the storm. People were still cleaning up debris and fallen branches, and some roads were still blocked off because of flooding.

"Seems like we always have important conversations when we're in the car, like when Gabriel called me the other day about the job posting. I think we need to have an important conversation now, to discuss Maria and Amy's roles and what our expectations are for them when they manage the bed-and-breakfast for us," suggested Nicole.

"Good idea. How about the first step, let's name our business?" asked Lia. "By the way, we're going to have to meet with our lawyer, I mean boyfriend, Drew Blackburn, soon to do all the legal paperwork for the business."

"Oh, please. Don't get me started. I already feel guilty that he seems to enjoy speaking with me so much."

"What about the fact that you enjoy speaking with him, at times?" asked Lia.

Nicole winced. "Please don't make me feel worse. Maybe if things improve with Dean, I will feel better about my relationship with him. It must be that I'm not getting something from our relationship that I really need. Anyway, let's get back to business!"

"Okay," said Lia, raising her eyebrows.

"Hmm. How about we keep it simple?" Nicole paused, rubbing her chin. "'Waterford House'? And we can add 'A Historic Inn' on the sign outside and on the website, sort of like a subtitle."

"Well, it's simple. But effective. If people search online for a place to stay in Waterford, it will certainly be right at the top! And it clearly explains it's a historic house; some people are seeking that in particular. Always good to make things as easy as possible for people!" said Lia, winking at Nicole while they were at a stop sign.

"That's your great business sense talking! Okay, next steps. We need to discuss roles and responsibilities for Amy and Maria. I think the primary responsibilities will be front desk service, establishing the menu and preparing the food, and managing the staff," suggested

Nicole. "And I think we ought to suggest that they work together to draw up plans on how much cleaning staff or anyone else they might need, and have them propose the plan to us. They can take part in the planning and hiring so they feel more ownership."

"All good points, Nicole!" remarked Lia as they pulled up in front of the property.

Nicole was pleased to see that the water had mostly receded in the area near the house. Once they parked in front and exited Lia's car, Nicole noticed Tommy's truck was still at the house, but did not see any other vehicles. She assumed the Sorria sisters had not arrived yet.

After going through the front door, Nicole was shocked to see Maria and Amy standing in the foyer! Nicole surmised they must have parked further away or around the corner. "Hi Maria and Amy!" Nicole admired her cousin Maria's appearance. Maria was very tall and lean, with gorgeous blonde hair that went past her shoulders. And Amy Sorria, her twin sister, was short and round, with black hair in a bob hairstyle. You'd never know these two were sisters, let alone twins, but they were, in fact, fraternal twins.

And they could not be more different in personality, to boot.

"Cousin Nicole!" Maria jumped and practically leapt over her sister Amy to hug Nicole. "And Lia, so great to see you too!" Since Lia had grown up very close to Nicole and her family, they all knew each other fairly well.

Amy, a bit more subdued, barely uttered an audible "hello" and gave a quick hug to both Nicole and Lia.

"Thank you, ladies, for coming! Especially after the storm. You guys get here okay?" asked Nicole.

"Yes, we made it here fine from the city. Can't wait to get out of there and move in *here*. This place is incredible! Can you give us the grand tour?" asked Maria.

Amy and Maria Sorria previously owned their own catering business in New York City, but they were happy to dissolve that business for a quieter life in New Jersey. The stress of catering large events had been wearing on them, and they were looking forward to the opportunity to join forces with Nicole in the bed-and-breakfast business. Since they could very easily prepare delicious breakfasts and meals for guests, and since they liked the idea of free room and board, they jumped on the opportunity when Nicole presented it.

"Let's go, ladies. I'll take you through the first

floor and show you where we expect to place the reception desk, how we'll arrange the dining room, and so forth. The second floor is complete with renovated bedrooms and private bathrooms installed. And Tommy is probably upstairs now working on the third floor storage attic area." Nicole waved them on. As the four ladies took their time inspecting the house, Lia and Nicole talked about the expectations for their respective roles in managing the Waterford House.

"I can't wait to come back and stay here one night! And I'm already getting so many ideas about the menus!" said Maria. She was practically squealing.

Amy, who was mostly quiet throughout the tour, groaned loudly. "There she goes again! Fantasizing about the future! Now we need to stay firm, Maria, this time around. We got too fanciful in our last business and we got overwhelmed real fast. Okay, sister?" Amy had a bit of a grumpy face on while Maria rolled her eyes and shook her head. Lia and Nicole glanced at each other, both thinking the same thing. These two couldn't be more different!

CHAPTER TWELVE

"WELL, today should be an interesting day at the library. Don't you think?" asked Lia. She and Nicole were sitting at Nicole's kitchen table. Once again, they were discussing a murder mystery over breakfast. But this time it was about a murder that happened a hundred years ago! Nicole bent over to pet Ringo before he went through the doggie door in the kitchen.

"Indeed. I think it's interesting that both Neelam and Beth will join us. I wonder what that dynamic is going to be like?" mused Nicole. She set her coffee cup down and cocked her head, lost in thought.

"I do find it interesting that Beth decided to join us. It's not so surprising about Neelam, especially given our history with her. And hey, this is a great opportunity to ask Beth to join us for the next Downtown Management meeting. We promised the mayor, didn't we?" said Lia. Lia took Nicole's plate and her own and set them in the sink. "Ready? I'll drive!"

"I was hoping you would say that, silly!" The ladies laughed. Nicole poked her head out the back door to tell Ringo she was on her way out. He came running up to her feet, barking. She pet him one more time and then proceeded out the front door with Lia into her SUV. After a quick dash across town, they parked in the lot. At 10 AM in the summer, the library was not terribly busy; though Nicole recalled from her high school years of working part-time in the children's department that parents would start trickling in with their children as the day wore on, especially once their summer camps completed for the day.

"Maybe I should have become a librarian," said Nicole, rubbing her forehead.

"Is this about that university job again? How would you help students if you became a librarian?" asked Lia. She lightly touched Nicole's arm to gesture for them to walk over, slowly. There were a few patrons waiting outside, so the doors must have still been locked, Nicole assumed.

"I'm feeling very stressed about this opportunity that came up after all. If I go back to the university, I'm going to get consumed by the environment and all the issues there. I should focus on our new Waterford House and the Cannoli Cafe instead. I mean, do you want us to fail at this new business?" Nicole's eyes glistened when she asked Lia her questions. She felt so conflicted, especially since she missed teaching her students, not to mention the fact that the job posting was truly her dream job — now that she had a chance to review the posting.

"Hey," said Lia softly. They stopped walking. "What is the actual issue here with the job? You know, Nicole, you can do whatever you want."

"I'm just very confused about what the best path forward is for me. But all I can do right now is pray about it and have faith that everything will work out. All the stress thinking about the new opportunity isn't going to help us be successful with this bed-and-breakfast. And right now, our goal is to solve this mystery. Like it or not, we need to put this case to bed, no pun intended. And, for good measure, we will ensure that there are no ghostly dreams or sightings by our guests in our new house, as long as we solve this thing!"

"Okay, Nicole. Then let's go solve this thing! Oh, I see Neelam on the other side of the building, approaching the front door. Let's go meet her!" said Lia as they picked up the pace.

Nicole waved over to them. "Hi Neelam! How's Jason?" asked Nicole.

The ladies exchanged hugs before Neelam answered. "That boy is certainly keeping me busy! I think I'm running out of energy!" Everyone chuckled as Neelam twirled her long, black hair. Nicole noticed how it shined beautifully in the sunlight that morning. Suddenly, Edna, a longtime employee of the library, unlocked and opened the front doors. "Where's Beth? Has anyone seen her?" asked Neelam.

"Not yet. But maybe we should go find Christina, and if Beth comes in, she can find us inside the library," suggested Lia.

"Sounds like a plan!" said Neelam.

The three ladies smiled at one another and joined together, arm in arm, as they approached the front door. Just like when they were eight years old. After walking inside, they found Christina Morano, the director of the library. Christina also happened to be the wife of Dan Morano, manager of her aunt's restaurant in town, *Lucia's Trattoria*.

After the ladies exchanged pleasantries, Christina said, "Thank you for your text yesterday. I already did some digging, and I've got a bunch of articles prepared for you in the back room. Let's go!"

As the ladies pored over the articles that were printed from the digitized archives, Nicole scoured for any clues she could find. She found other photos of Jack Dixon with Herman Hammond and Frederick Clemmons, but not much else. Disappointed that she could not find anything new or relevant to the case, she started to think they were going to come up empty. Although, perhaps Tommy, back at the house, could get through that wall in the kitchen and find that secret basement. At least that could be something!

Suddenly, Beth walked in holding something carefully in her hands.

"Ladies, I need to tell you something." She paused and inhaled a deep breath. "I am the great-granddaughter of Melba Dixon. And this was her jewelry box!"

CHAPTER THIRTEEN

THE WOMEN all stared at each other in disbelief — Nicole, Christina, Lia, and Neelam. "Wait a second, Beth. Can you repeat that?" asked Nicole.

Beth looked down and crossed her right foot over her left foot, appearing bashful. "I said I am the great-granddaughter of Melba Dixon, and this is her jewelry box." Beth then looked up and stared at everyone with her wide blue eyes.

"Is that why you moved here a couple years ago, Beth? Because technically you are related to the famous Jack Dixon?" asked Nicole. There was silence in the room, to the point where you could hear a pin drop. Everyone waited on bated breath for Beth's response.

Beth, her eyes glistening, said, "Yes. I wanted a

new start here, and I wanted to see if I could find out more about my ancestry. I had heard all these stories growing up about how my great grandfather, Jack Dixon, was murdered — yet no one knew how or why. I was secretly hoping for answers and to get reconnected to this area. My grandfather, Robert Dixon, died alone. And my mother did not want the house he willed her. She never claimed it before she died herself." Beth paused, looking down again at her feet. "You see, my mother, Mary Dixon Wendell, had moved to Pennsylvania when she was eighteen years old. She lived a very quiet life when she was here briefly in Rosewood in the 1950s and 60s. But she was also so haunted by all the talk of Jack Dixon and his murder that she wanted a fresh start, so she moved to Pennsylvania as soon as she could."

"Wow. This is major," said Lia.

Christina started to pace in the room, rubbing her chin. "That would make sense as to why the house was essentially abandoned. And I could not find much in terms of Robert's descendents in the articles. I suppose your mother led a very quiet life. There wasn't anything published about her. Perhaps the township had a birth certificate, but we didn't get that far in our investigation."

Neelam shook her head in agreement. They really had not gotten too far in terms of searching ancestry, especially since they were still so focused on the house itself and the history with moonshine and the store.

"Wait a second!" said Neelam, her face tight. "So all this time we've been talking about the case this week, you just let us talk and you don't say anything! Until now? At the cafe, you told us you wanted to help us investigate, but you neglected to tell us why!" Nicole watched as she saw Neelam's anger bubble up. "You misled us!"

Nicole's eyes widened as she recognized Neelam's impassioned personality coming to the surface. She was not one to hide behind the truth! And she often called people on their misdeeds.

Beth looked down and rubbed her hands together after placing the box on the table beside her. She said, "Yes, I'm sorry. I did not mean to mislead you. It's just that I was starting to enjoy my life here as a new person, and was not quite ready to disclose my ancestry. But now that this is going on — and Nicole and Lia need help solving this mystery, so that their ghostly apparitions, or any issues related to the bed-and-breakfast can dissipate — I feel it's important for me to tell you the truth.

And that's why I've brought you this jewelry box. I thought perhaps some of the contents could lead to some insight that I have not uncovered yet."

Nicole looked at Christina, Neelam, and Lia and nodded to them. She was often the peace-keeper during disputes. She hoped they could move on from talk of being misled and move on to solving the mystery. "Okay, Beth. We appreciate you coming forward. May we take a look?" said Nicole.

Beth's face brightened at Nicole's gesture and words. "Yes, please!" She slid the box over in their direction. The other three women approached the table. Nicole took the lead and carefully opened the box. Inside, she found pearls, rings, earrings, and brooches. Then she also noticed a small book at the bottom of the box.

"Hey, what's this?" she asked.

"I looked at it in the past, but it just seems like a bunch of little poems or sayings. My great-grand-mother must have written them. And my mother, who took this box in her possession upon Great-Grandmother Melba's passing, didn't know anything about it," answered Beth.

Nicole quickly sifted through the poetry book and then passed it around to the other women to see what they thought. Once they each inspected it for a few minutes, it made its way back to Nicole. After paging through the book once more, Nicole suddenly gasped and said, "I think this might be a clue. Excellent! Here, listen to this!" Nicole proceeded to say the poem aloud, which read:

Heavy, heavy rods bearing light,

Might you save my life tonight,

My life is more than a beating heart,

My family legacy is my true life, my true heart.

"This sounds like she was in some sort of danger! Maybe someone was targeting the family? Perhaps she knew who the murderer was or suspected somebody was going to come after them!" said Christina, clearly intrigued. Nicole then remembered the obscure reference to Raymond Ackerman in the second dream she had the other night.

"Well, it is certainly a mystery!" said Lia.

Everyone chuckled, the tension in the air thinning. "Oh, Lia!" said Nicole and Neelam in unison.

CHAPTER FOURTEEN

"Okay, okay, okay, ladies! You gotta see this! And Nicole, you were on to something." said Tommy. Nicole and Lia glanced over to the kitchen wall that was previously solid. Now, a gaping hole led to some very dusty, old stairs leading to a dark room below. Nicole and Lia nodded to each other. "Here, let me lead the way for you. I have the special lantern here." As Tommy led the way with his beacon of sorts, Lia and Nicole stayed very close behind. They very carefully went down what felt like a dark, secret passage. When they finally reached the bottom of the stairs, they found a massive secret room!

"Does this look like your dream, Nicole?" asked Lia.

"You dreamt this?" asked Tommy. "You gotta be kidding me!"

"Eh, it was just a hunch!" Nicole took Lia's hand, worried she might lose her footing in the dark. She was also prone to dizzy spells, at times, and did not want to take any chances with the hard floor below. "Now, let's keep going! Is there a door that could possibly lead to another place or another property?" Nicole glanced around the room. Dark, and bare, it did not look much like what she had seen, since the entire distillery operation was removed! At that moment, Nicole surmised that Frederick Clemmons most likely relocated all the equipment through the secret passage to his property. If only they could find that door!

Tommy felt around the walls slowly. He kept shaking his head, seeming unconvinced that there were any doors down there. Suddenly, he yelled, "Hey! There is something here! But it's all boarded up. I'm afraid to open it. What if it does some structural damage? I don't think I have enough insurance to cover me for that. There could be a cave-in or something! But there's definitely something here, Nicole."

"Thanks, Tommy, that's all I needed to know! We can head upstairs now," said Nicole.

"So, what do you want to do with this place? Storage?" asked Tommy as he led them back up the stairs.

"Do you think you and your guys can figure out how to turn it into a game room?" asked Nicole.

"That's a great idea. And we do have money in the budget. If you're worried about us paying, Tommy!" said Lia.

"Sounds like a plan to me! I'll get my guys working on it next week. Especially now that we're done with most of the house. By the way, did you want to check out the attic again? I rewired it so there's more light; you can see better now!" said Tommy as he waited for the ladies at the top of the stairs.

"Sounds like a great idea! Lia, let's head upstairs now. Tommy, feel free to stay down here as long as you need. Lia and I are going to stay overnight after we check out the attic again," said Nicole.

As Lia and Nicole headed upstairs, Nicole took the opportunity to compare the 1920s version of the house in her memory (from the dreams) with her current house. There was certainly a lot more wallpaper back then, but the woodwork was identical, just fresher seeming in the 1920s. And of course 1920s music wasn't playing now either, although it did give her an idea to possibly play 1920s music in the foyer/lobby with the sound system for guests, to add to the historic ambiance. But then again, she wondered if playing 1920s music was going too far, perhaps making the ghosts feel a bit too welcome! She chuckled to herself.

"Penny for your thoughts, Nicole?" asked Lia.

"Nah, this one is not worth sharing!" replied Nicole. As they made their way up to the third floor, Nicole reflected on how differently the attic looked with lights on, especially with the last bit of sunlight trickling in through the windows. Suddenly, she noticed the two large candlesticks again. "Wait a second!" She ran over to the candlesticks and held them up. These would look great downstairs! I think they are silver-plated. I can clean these and they would be great in the dining room!"

"That's a great idea! Now see anything else you want to check out?" asked Lia.

Nicole spent some time going through the chests again in the attic, and Lia looked at the photos once again, but they basically came up with nothing new. Nicole reviewed the letters once again, just to make sure she didn't miss clues or hints, especially now that had the dreams in the back of her mind for context. After taking their time in the attic, and when the sunlight grew dim, they decided it was time to head to bed. At least this time, they were prepared with pajamas and things to amuse themselves with while they fell asleep. Nicole had brought a book to read, and Lia had actually brought some of her accounting paperwork to work on. Once they retired to their respective rooms once again, Nicole braced herself for yet another night. She hoped this was the last time she'd have any ghostly apparitions or dreams, anyway.

As she finally drifted off to sleep, once again, she woke up what felt like an hour later. She could tell she was back in the 1920s based on the slight change in how the room appeared. The coat rack was again in the corner. She raised herself from the bed and grabbed the robe. This time, it was very unclear how she should proceed through the house. She did not hear any music, nor did the translucent Jack Dixon meet her anywhere. She took her time exploring while a violent storm was occurring outside the windows. Thunder blooming and lightning flashing, it was very similar to the night she experienced earlier that week when Lia and Nicole had gotten trapped.

As she made her way around the rooms, Nicole decided to go inside Lia's bedroom, curious to see if her friend was inside after all. She opened the door and gasped. The study! She saw 1920s Jack Dixon pacing inside near his desk. Her heartbeat quickened as she suddenly realized she was about to witness the murder of Jack Dixon and solve the mystery!

She carefully went further into the room and watched as Jack Dixon continued to pace across the room, going back-and-forth and mumbling to himself. Goosebumps rose from her flesh as she started to hyperventilate. She couldn't believe she was about to witness a murder. She watched Jack as he sat down at his desk and wrote the three suspects' names down. Then he got up once again and before she knew it, a dark, cloaked figure dashed into the room and grabbed two candlesticks off the fireplace! Suddenly, in that moment, she remembered the poem from Melba Dixon's jewelry box and how the verses read as, *"Heavy, heavy rods bearing light, might you save my life tonight."*

In that moment, Nicole realized Melba Dixon was not saving herself from a stranger or intruder, but she was saving her family life and legacy. From what she considered ruin — the moonshine business!

Instinctively, Nicole shouted at the figure

completely covered in black. "Stop, Melba, stop!"
Immediately, the entire room disintegrated into
blackness, and the translucent Jack Dixon
approached Nicole and said, "Thank you, my dear.
While I am disheartened that it was Melba, I
needed to know and face the truth. After all, a part
of me knew that it was her deep down, but I
needed to be sure. But I'm now ready to move on,
and I thank you for that."

And just then, Jack floated away up to the
heavens as Nicole stared after him in utter disbelief.

CHAPTER FIFTEEN

"Nicole, why do I get the sense that there's something you're not telling me about this job situation?" asked Gabriel. He was sitting across from Nicole at one of the small bistro tables inside the Cannoli Cafe.

"I was ready to move on with my life outside the university from teaching part-time. But now that this Professor of Practice posting exists, I need closure. I need to see where it could go." She sniffled. "I just don't want to wonder, *what if?* Besides, I'm truly fascinated by the role itself. I think I would actually enjoy it, and could really make a difference for the students."

"So there are some emotions involved here. What are you going to do? What is your very next step, dear?" asked Gabriel. He gripped his mug and looked across to her, squinting out of curiosity. Nicole could smell the peppermint tea from across the table.

"I'm going to start working on my application tomorrow. And continue to pray about it, as well," said Nicole firmly.

"I think your plan is good. Taking action always helps relieve the pain of uncertainty and resistance. Stick with that! So, perhaps you were meant to go back there, after all, or maybe it's just wishful thinking on my part." He smiled. "In the meantime, let's toast to you solving the mystery of who killed the famous Jack Dixon! And cheers to opening up your new Waterford House in the coming weeks!" They clinked mugs, and Nicole blinked back tears, feeling so grateful for her dear and wise friend from the University of New Jersey.

Just then, Mr. Martini called Nicole over. He and Max were setting up a huge table to celebrate another mystery solved in Rosewood! Nicole and Gabriel got up from their small table and made their way over to the big one. "Now, sit here next to me, okay Nicole?" said Max.

"Sure thing, Max," answered Nicole as she affectionately tapped him on the arm. Everyone smiled. As Nicole gazed around the table, she saw all her dear friends: Aunt Lucia and Vince Mongelli, the Knitting for Good ladies, Max and Mr. Don Martini, Lia, Neelam, and even Beth.

Beth stood up and approached Nicole's chair. "Nicole, I just want to thank you for your help the other day at the library. I'm sorry I misled you — unintentionally, of course — but I'm hopeful, now that the case is behind us, to keep in touch."

Nicole could sense the sincerity in Beth's voice. She nodded. "Of course. Actually, we were so shocked by your news the other day, that we forgot to invite you to join us at the next Downtown Management meeting. I can email or text you the information, if you'd like?" asked Nicole.

Beth beamed. "Now, that sounds wonderful!" After exchanging phone numbers, Beth returned to her seat, especially once she noticed what was about to happen. Susie and Celeste, one of the servers at the cafe, came out from the back with trays of coffees, cannolis, and cookies for everyone. As everyone rose to dive into the assortment, they turned to see who was coming through the front door of the cafe.

"Oh! Dean!" Nicole jumped up and approached the cafe door. Dean walked in and immediately approached Nicole, giving her a big hug and a kiss on the lips. The whole cafe applauded and cheered in the background.

"Oh, is this my retirement party? How'd you know?" asked Dean. He adjusted his glasses before pulling his strong hands through his thick, black hair.

"Retirement party?" Nicole looked at Dean in disbelief. "You really retired from the FBI? For real, this time?" Nicole's eyes flooded, and suddenly her cheeks were full of tears.

Nicole knew what that meant. Dean was choosing her, after all.

Life was about to get a lot more interesting in the coming months for Nicole, with the return of her beau, her new business at the Waterford House, and possibly the continuation of her novel — if she did not get the Professor of Practice role, of course. Her eyes still glistening, she gave Dean another hug, and the whole cafe stayed abuzz in all the excitement. Lia winked over at Nicole, and she winked back with a huge grin. The Cannoli Cafe was certainly the place to be that warm, sunny afternoon in the charming town of Rosewood, New Jersey.

AUTHOR'S NOTE

The Cannoli Cafe Mystery Series is inspired by my Italian-American upbringing in New Jersey (my mother's family is Italian and I grew up very close to them; I spent a lot of time at my grandparents' house when I was a child, enjoying traditional Italian cooking).

While the aforementioned elements are true of my own life, the entire story and all the characters are fictional, and any coincidences to any particular events or anything else are just that—coincidental and fictional.

I sincerely hope you enjoyed my seventh work of fiction, and if you'd like to be notified when my next book comes out, please visit:

http://lizziebenton.com.

Also, you are welcome to follow my Goodreads Author Page .

Thank you again for reading!

www.ingramcontent.com/pod-product-compliance
Lightning Source LLC
Chambersburg PA
CBHW061349160726
47995CB00001B/237